Li'L Roar Dinosaur

Goes to Camp

V.S. Srinivas

To Nitro – My two little superheroes!

Original sketches by V.S. Srinivas

Li'l Roar Dinosaur Goes to Camp

Story & Concept

V.S. Srinivas

Illustrations

Rohini Sadasivan

About the Author

V.S. Srinivas loved to doodle, draw and think up cool stories when he got some time from his busy schedule as a cardiologist in New York. Srinivas wrote this book to help his twins settle into camp. Srinivas' vivid imagination and artistic talent is evident through this delightful story.

Acknowledgements

Special thanks to Arun – Convex Studios for all his help with making this book a reality.

Published by

Notion Press

Old No. 38, New No. 6
McNichols Road, Chetpet
Chennai - 600 031
First Published by Notion Press 2015

ISBN: 978-93-5206-295-9

DINO CAMP

Li'l Roar Dinosaur loved camp!

At Camp, all the dinosaurs swam, played games,
ate snacks, napped,

played more games and took the school bus home.

But Li'l Roar Dinosaur

splashed too much water,

spilled his snacks and

roared during nap time
and frightened the other campers.

The camp teachers tried to get Li'l Roar to behave. They talked to him, but he closed his ears.

They rewarded good behavior hoping he would learn,
but Li'l Roar did not care.

They removed him from the other campers at naptime, but he made noises anyway. Nothing helped.

So the camp counselor called mommy dinosaur to take Li'l Roar out of camp.

Li’l Roar Dinosaur was sad.
Now he could not swim, play games
or share snacks with the other campers.

Suddenly Li'l Roar

Dinosaur had an **idea!**

He said to mommy dinosaur “How about if I don’t splash, roar or make noises? May I go to camp then?”

"Sure. But how will you make sure you behave well?" mommy dinosaur asked.

"Simple!" said Li'l Roar.
"Before I start any activity,
I will remind myself the rules."

Mommy Dinosaur said
“That’s a good idea!
Let me talk to the counselor.”

The next day, Li'l Roar Dinosaur woke up,

drank his milk,
had his breakfast,

and took the bus to camp.

At camp,
he swam, but did not splash.

He snacked, but did not spill.

He played games and was a good sport.
He ate lunch and did not waste.

He napped and did not make noises.

The counselor was happy,
the camp teachers were happy, the other campers were happy,

and most importantly,

Li'l Roar Dinosaur was a **happy camper!**

More original sketches by V.S. Srinivas